ZANY HUMOR FOR ELVES, IMPS AND CLOWNS

"The Alley Cat of Jokes"

BUDDY ALLEY

authorHOUSE®

AuthorHouse™
1663 Liberty Drive
Bloomington, IN 47403
www.authorhouse.com
Phone: 1 (800) 839-8640

Published by AuthorHouse 06/25/2016

ISBN: 978-1-5246-0104-1 (sc)
ISBN: 978-1-5246-1327-3 (e)

Library of Congress Control Number: 2016904875

Print information available on the last page.

Contents

DEDICATION

To My Parents - Rodney and May Alley -- and my Little Sister Shirley

I was born to Rodney and May Alley while they were tourning with a company of actors in Moline, Illinois. They were known for their imitations, dancing, and comedy routines -- both on state and backstage.

Before her marriage my mother May Hirshmann worked in Burlesque as a stripper. She was called "the Powder Puff Gal." Why? Because she came on stage only covered by a large powder puff. Her act consisted of throwing out small powder puffs so that the men in the audience could powder various parts of her beautiful body.

My dad Rodney was a stand-up comic and appeared in various "joints" in all parts of the country. He was especially known for his one-liners. His comedy style was very much like that of Henny Youngman.

After they were married they tourned as a couple and entertained people with their songs, dancing and repartees.

As a child I joined them on stage to dance, sing and exchange funny lines. My sister Shirley joined the act at the age of four. Later I went out on my own as a stand-up and my sister became night club singer under the name Diana Lamore.

We both loved our parents dearly. Tragically, both were killed in an airplane crash while touring to entertain our troops.

SHOULD YOU BUY THIS BOOK?

If you answer "yes" to the following, you should. You will find it a hoot.

1. You smile when you read the following names:

   Milton Berle

   Sid Ceaser and Imogene Coca

   Harpo Marx

   Bob Hope

   Red Skelton

   Carol Burnet

   Mae West

   Lucille Ball

2. You recognize the following lead-in to a joke:

   "How does a blonde..."

   "Yo momma's so ugly..."

   "What do you call..."

   "Mommy, mommy, can..."

   "Knock, knock..."

3. You enjoy reading poems by Ogden Nash and Garrison Keillor.

4. You have a large collection of joke books.

5. You laugh at the following cartoons:

   Marmaduke

   Mother Goose and Grimm

   Beetle Bailey

1

For Better Or Worse

6. You love to see again and again the following films:

    <u>Night at the Opera</u>

    <u>Some Like It Hot</u>

    <u>Blazing Saddles</u>

7. You love to see re-runs of the following TV shows:

    <u>The Golden Girls</u>

    <u>The Carol Burnet Show</u>

    <u>I Love Lucy</u>

8. You like to dress your pet in funny outfits.

9. You know what they do at the Friars Club.

10. You laugh at the following illustrations because you have used them to make fun of others.

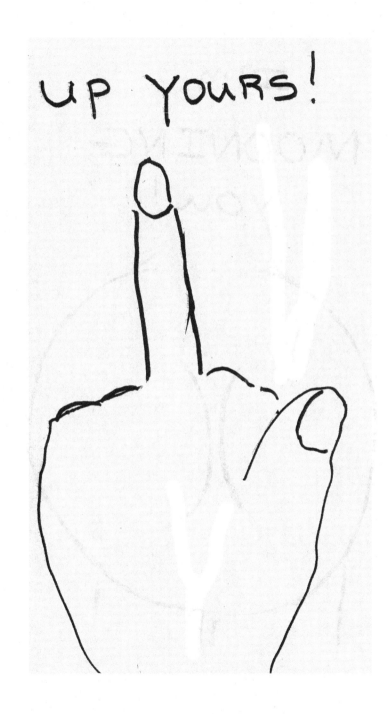

A MESSAGE FROM BUDDY ALLEY

Hi there! So happy to greet a fellow clown like myself. It is very difficult being one these days -- especially in the workplace. Too many evaluations and hidden listening and viewing devices to having fun and pulling pranks on the job. Yes, these days it takes courage to be a clown, elf or imp.

You decided to buy this book because you feel as I do that laughter is good for the soul. Indeed, it brightens up our days. Most clowns feel that a good belly-laugh a day, keeps the doctor away.

All the words in the dictionary reflect the topics and techniques of comedians. Being a clown myself, I often could not resist the urge to pull your leg just for laughs.

I'm sure that you love humor in all its forms --- jokes, funny stories, one-liners, pranks, imitations and role-playing.

Many of us enjoy naughty humor. So, watch out dear reader. Be prepared for some surprises. Yes, you may come upon a word or even an entire routine that many of your relatives may call "raunchy." But, being a clown, you will love them.

As you start reading this book, I wish you a happy trip down the road that only an imp, elf or clown can appreciate. I hope that the special features will especially give you plenty of smiles, giggles and belly-laughs.

Now start reading and looking. Enjoy!

COMIC WORDS FROM A TO Z

A

Rosie Asshoffer:

"I still get a giggle whenever I see a Woody Allen or a Fatty Arbuckle film."

THE TOP TEN As

aback --
to be surprised when you look behind you and find someone about to do something naughty. Favorite type of body humor found in adult comic shows and films.

ad-lib --
The ability to improvise whenever anything goes amiss. Red Skelton and Sid Caesar were good at it.

accessory --
a G-string over your tunnel of love or cock.

acquiesce --
to lower onself to meet the needs of one's lover. Used in naughty comedy bits.

acrobat --
a performer of incredible sexual positions. Used in adult x-rated shows.

adaptable --
the ability to become male/female when the situation requires it.

addictive --
a lust to do the "forbidden." Often given to a character in a comedy show.

armed --
one is equipped with condoms and hence ready for action. Used in risque comedy scenes.

anti --
Being against something. A comic character would often do this to the extreme. Archie Bunker in <u>All In The Family</u> was such a character. Makes for a lot of laughs.

automaton --
a mechanism that is relatively self-operating - a robot. Such items are often used in comedy scenes.

B

Kissy Balls

"Nothing gives me a belly-laugh faster than seeing Lucille Ball or Milton Berle do slapstick."

THE TOP TEN Bs

Bacchus --
: The Greek god of wine who is often featured in wild comedy party scenes.

bad ass --
: ready to cause or get into trouble. Many comedy skits must have this type of character to get the plot rolling.

baloney --
: pretentious nonsense -- an element essential to comedy. Often used to refer to a man's cock in R rated routines.

banged --
: again often used as a slang term meaning "I've made love."

baptism --
: often used to indicate the first time that a comic has been hit in the face with a pie.

bareback --
: very nasty humor - the act of riding one's lover without saddle -- usually gets a big laugh with the right audience. Gays laugh at guys who do not use condoms.

base runner --
: winning the lady or man at the end of the comedy show after much foreplay and misadventures.

baths --
: places where one often finds more than hot water, steam and a friendly chat -- x-rated show.

beehive --
: refers to a scene where there are many actors involved in some funny action; it can also refer (in a X-rated show) to a lady's pussy that is surrounded and attacked by many a horny guy.

C

Lola Climax:

"If anyone can get a smile and a laugh out of me its Johnny Carson talking with Tiny Tim or Sid Caesar doing a bit with Imogene Coca. It's always a hoot to watch them in action."

THE TOP TEN Cs

caboose --   a word often used by comics in speaking about one's butt -- often followed by a pinch or slap.

capsize --   a favorite physical comic device used to get laughs -- a boat or something capsizes.

caravan --   a traveling group of clowns who put on shows at small towns.

contest --   a favorite setting for a comic routine -- it's usually a beauty or dancing contest.

crafty --   the use of cunning and guile -- often an essential part of a funny character's behavior -- usually backfires on him or her.

crying --   an old device used in comical situation -- the crying must be done well to result in laughter. Lucy did it a lot on I Love Lucy.

crystal ball --   a prop often used in comic scenes -- involves comic playing a fortune teller, and seeing weird events.

cuckoo --   slang term often used to indicate that a character is irrational -- not with it -- usually the person making the remark uses his/her finger in a circular manner by the head to drive home the point.

cue --   every comic knows that he must always be on cue with a remark or movement for the gag to work.

cum --   basically semen. Used now by directors of gay porn for a funny scene. Instead of the actor getting a pie in his face, he gets semen. It's very funny to the right audience.

D

Hardy Dick:

"Those one-liners from Rodney Dangerfield are so over the top. And, Jimmy Durante's nose makes me giggle. He doesn't even have to say anything."

TOP TEN Ds

dancing -- comics often dance together in unison or in a funny way to get laughs. The cast of <u>Are</u> <u>You</u> <u>Being</u> <u>Served</u> did it a lot.

dialects -- comics tell stories in various dialects for laughs -- e.g. Irish, Yiddish, etc.

dingbat -- a word used to suggest that the person is off their heads -- totally out of it.

doing -- at work, walking, dancing, -- person is in motion.

dong-- word used to refer to penis -- used a lot in R-rated comedy.

doo-doo -- a term relating to shitting -- used in naughty humor relating to bodily functions.

dreams -- often used as a setting for a funny scene-- comic does wild things in them.

drunk -- comics often play characters who have had one too many.

dumbhead -- appears in many jokes about certain groups -- blondes, Poles, etc.

dumbstruck -- a favorite type of body humor used to get the audience to pay attention and laugh.

dummy -- this can refer to puppets or as a word to describe a person who isn't with it.

dwarf -- many Wee people often get laughs by being in a routine -- goes back centuries -- when dwarfs do certain things -- running, skipping it seems funnier.

E

Mark Eatmee:

"Tom Ewell's face expressions in <u>The Seven Year Itch</u> made me smile. He was great with Marilyn Monroe."

THE TOP TEN Es

earthy -- telling naughty stories or jokes.

edge -- going to the edge in a skit to get a lot of laughs from the audience -- could be the edge of a roof, etc.

eggs -- the things that even bad comics don't want thrown at them.

ego -- something that every comic must have to go on with a routine night after night.

elasticity -- what a comic's face must have in order to keep the audience laughing.

embellish -- what every comic knows he or she must do to make a tale really funny.

eye -- different positions of the eye ball can express different comic emotions -- very essential part of physical comedy.

Emmy -- what every comic hopes to win so he can keep working on a situation comedy show.

Emu -- a bird with a strange walk-- comics become them and dress up like one to get laughs.

encounter -- an element that is in most comic scenes -- comic meets or runs into wife, mother-in-law, boss, wall etc.

F

Glorius Feel:

"I always remember seeing Mae West and W.C. Fields play-off the clever double entendres. Together they were a riot."

THE TEN TOP Fs

face --   the part of the human body that comics use the most to get laughs.

fart --   this bodily function always gets a laugh. Sophia on the Golden Girls did it a lot and got plenty of laughs.

fat --   often used by comics to get a laugh -- e.g. "your mama is as fat as..."

fetish --   a topic that is often used in jokes -- hats, toes, feet, butts, etc.

field --   to a comic it is used for jokes involving dating, playing the field --e.g. dos and don't on the first date.

flat --   falling flat on your face gets giggles and laughs -- but it is hard on comics -- broken bones etc.

flip-flop --   another device of physical humor -- often comics become seals, fish, etc.

foozle --   to get a laugh by managing to playing awkwardly -- walking or running in a wild crazy way:

foreplay --   great part of comedy involving couples-- used in naughty humor -- kissing, feeling, doing "no-nos."

free-wheeling --   what every good comic learns --to be funny you can't be restrained by any rules.

G

Peter Gigantic:

"I loved all the funny characters that Jackie Gleason came up with. His slapstick was the best."

THE TOP TEN Gs

gag --   a joke - a laugh provoking remark.

gale --   something every comic hopes will happen when his routine goes over well -- an emotional outburst of laughter.

gamy --   what some comics specialize in to a dirty-minded audience -- the material is sexually suggestive.

gang --   the word that is often used in describing a group of comic actors -- e.g. Our Gang, etc.

garb --   another word for the costumes and props that comics wear to get into character and make people laugh.

gasbag --   often a loveable but talkative comic character-- e.g. Mrs. Gladys Kravits, Aunt Clara.

genitalia --   X-R rated jokes are often about the "private parts" of the human bodies -- many find jokes about penises, vulvas, butt-holes hilarious.

genteel --   the upper-class woman who is very proper --e.g. Margaret Dumont played such a character with the Marx Brothers.

gibberish --   device by comics to get laughs -- they employ meaningless language in their routines

gender --   male/female-- comics like to play drag--e.g. Milton Berle. Often comediennes play men to get laughs. Lucy on I Love Lucy did it a lot.

H

Ooso Hat:

Ooso Hat:

"Nobody could beat Bob Hope as an MC. His stinging comments of celebrities always brought down the house."

THE TOP TEN Hs

Ha! Ha! --   used to express amusement -- a comic's aim at entertaining.

half-assed --   often comic characters are persons (like Archie Bunker) who are funny because their ideas are so wrong.

half-pint --   again a comic character that is often short -- might have midget features.

ham --   a comic performer who exaggerates to get laughs -- a perhaps essential aspect of being a comic and liking to perform.

hand-puppet --   simple doll-like (even a sock over the hand with human features) that's used to get laughs -- usually from kids.

happy --   what a good laugh makes you feel.

happy-go-luck --   refers to many comic characters who appear totally unaware of any problem -- simple - minded -- but they are happy.

harlequin --   a character in comedy and pantomine with a shaved head, masked face, variegated-tights and wooden sword.

harp --   a prop used by Harpo Marx as part of his comic routine.

heckling --   the thing that comics fear -- that's why they pay "plants" in the audience to get the laughter going -- e.g. Berle's mom hired them for the great comic -- her son.

I

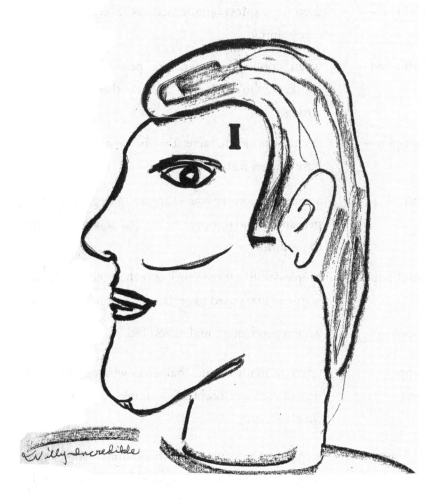

Willy Incredible

"Boy, that John Inman played the gay guy so well. And when he danced or dressed up in some far-out get-up, he stoled the show."

THE TOP TEN Is

ice --

many comical scenes take place on ice -- falling through the ice -- ice-skating on the ice, etc.

ice-cream --

great prop for slapstick comedy -- cone is pushed into someone's face -- scoops of ice-cream are arranged in an obscene way, etc.

if --

a short word that often starts a scene that leads to a funny answer or punch-line.

ignoramus --

a funny character that often appears in plays or TV shows -- Gracie Allen, Betty White can play dunces well.

illusionist --

a person who produces illusions that result in ohs, ahs and laughter.

imbecile --

a fool, idiot often found in plays by William Shakespeare and other writers.

immoral --

the subject of many jokes about sexual activities of call girls --- and just about every other animal or thing -- very R and X rated humor that is enjoyed by many people.

impish --

being very mischievous -- every comic really is an imp.

impregnate --

often an act found in R and X rated jokes about men and women.

intoxicate --

to get totally drunk -- often a device used by clowns and comics when doing their routines.

J

Quick Jackoff:

"Let's face it, Al Jolson not only could sing, but make people laugh. He had it all in terms of talent."

THE TOP TEN Js

jabber -- to talk rapidly, indistinctly or unintelligibly to get laughs.

jackass -- often a comic who is desperate for work will even play a donkey -- front or back end-- sometimes used to describe a character in a comical bit.

jam -- usually comic scenes involve characters who are in a bad situation -- how they deal with it makes an audience laugh.

Japanese -- often featured in ethnic jokes along with Jews and other ethnic groups.

jealous -- a human emotion that is often the basis of a humorous scene -- envy is great as a starting point for some very funny happenings.

Jekyil and Hyde -- this type of dual personality is often a device used in funny scenes and plots.

jerk -- a body movement often featured in slapstick-- also, it can describe some person who is really dumb or obnoxious.

jitter -- to be nervous -- a sense of panic -- irregular movements used a lot in physical comedy.

jokey -- given to being amusing -- some comics like Milton Berle never seem to be able to turn off their impish ways -- it becomes not only their profession to entertain but becomes the dominant part of the everyday person -- and not just their public persona.

K

Pussie Kissman:

"John Knott's eyes alone gave me a smile. They became the focus of the entire scene."

THE TEN TOP Ks

K -- The letter K has been found to cause laughter by comics. Hence, many characters have names that start with the letter K -- Kukla, Kaddiddlehopper, etc.

kangaroo -- often comics love to imitate this unusual Australian animal.

kerfuffle -- an aspect of body humor used by comics -- they become disheveled.

kick butt -- another favorite funny type of slapstick -- the audience loves to see someone get kicked in the ass - who knows why.

kidding -- a form of humor found among most nationalities-- for some reason people get a laugh out of giving someone a hard time about habits, hang-ups, etc.

kinky -- an unconventional taste or habit -- it often is an aspect of a comic character -- often found in R and X rated adult humor skits.

kiss and tell -- telling details of private matters -- a favorite device used in comedy shows.

kooky -- looking or acting offbeat or crazy -- an essential aspect of creating a funny character.

Kukla -- one of the funny puppets on the past TV show Kukla, Fran and Ollie.

kvetch -- used in Yiddish humor -- to squeeze, pinch -- a comic character may grip a lot.

L

Ahso Long:

"I loved to watch Harold Lloyd in silent films. His physical humor was as good as that of Charlie Chaplin's."

THE TOP TEN Ls

laughing gas --   nitrous oxide -- only used by comics when all other comic devices fail.

laughter --   the aim of all comics.

Laurel --   one of the great comics of all time -- he and his buddy Hardy made film shorts that are considered classics -- helped other hopefuls learn to be comedians.

lavatory --   another word for bathroom -- a setting for a lot of naughty humor.

lay --   a subject of many sexual jokes that some consider in poor taste -- others giggle with joy just hearing the word.

leapfrog --   one of many physical stunts used in stapstick comedy.

leer --   a lascivious knowing or wanton look often employed in comic scenes.

looney tunes --   funny cartoon characters that make kids and even adults laugh.

lewd --   a word used by those who dislike naughty humor.

libertine --   a person who is unrestrained by convention--such a person is often included in the players of TV comedy shows and plays -- e.g. Blanche in The Golden Girls, Blanche was after every good looking man and her bedroom was equipped with costumes, whips, video camera and a mirror on the ceiling.

M

Joe Macho:

"Those Marx brothers were great. They did one zany bit after another. Wow, what a team."

THE TOP TEN Ms

mace -- used for a temporary disabling -- often used as a prop in a comedy routine involving crooks.

machismo -- some comic character appears as an exaggerated person with a sense of power or strength.

mad and mad-cap -- used in many comic scenes where a character displays foolish, crazy behavior.

madam -- the female head of a house of prostitution -- a favorite character found in raunchy one-liners, jokes and naughty comedy.

make believe -- often used in comedy shows -- one or more of the characters becomes another person or thing.

make-out -- to engage in sexual intercourse -- often found in R and X rated scenes, jokes, one-liners.

malcontent -- used a lot -- the character isn't happy about something.

mispronounce -- characters say words incorrectly for a laugh, e.g. proposition becomes prostitution.

misuse -- a character becomes confused and uses words incorrectly, e.g. lesbian becomes Lebanese.

mystery -- often a setting for a comedy -- dinner mystery theatre, solving a crime, etc.

N

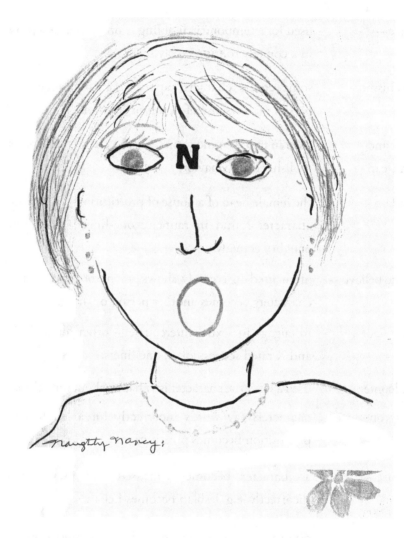

Naughty Nancy:

"Ozzie Nelson's humor was more quiet but still gave me and my friends a smile."

THE TEN TOP Ns

naughty --   being wicked or at least display implish behavior -- comic characters often have this aspect -- often used in dirty jokes about sex.

necking --   the art of kissing and caressing amorously - usually featured in plot-line for comedy shows.

neophyte --   a person who must be into the latest of everything -- clothes, shoes, slang, etc. Often a characteristic of a player in a farce.

nerd --   an inept person -- isn't with it socially -- many comics play such a person.

nerve --   what every comic must have to go out there and entertain -- especially if the audience is drunk-- having plenty of guts.

neurosis --   any type of emotional disorder -- usually some person in the cast has some weird behavior.

nightie --   prop used in funny bedroom scenes along with bras and panties-- often worn by men in drag roles -- very funny --ask Berle.

nimble --   to be quick and light in motion -- like Peter Pan --most comics can take on this style of movement.

nipple --   what would a sexy comedy be without doing or saying something about this part of a female or male body.

noodle --   to improvise on an instrument in a desultory manner -- often found in comedy -- especially by the Marx brothers.

O

Anus Open:

"Carroll O'Connor made "Archie" into an unforgettable comic personality."

THE TOP TEN Os

oaf --	a stupid person -- often used in comedy shows and jokes - "You're as stupied as..."
obese --	comics love the lead-in; "You're mama is as fat as..."
object --	often comics become things to the delight of an audience.
obliquity --	indirectness or deliberate obsecurity of speech or conduct -- takes great talent for a comic to pull it off.
obscenity --	most stand up comics depend on so-called "R" and "X" rated material -- the dirtier for many of them -- of course, you have to have the right audience.
obsession --	often comic characters are given unreasonable ideas or feelings to get laughs.
obstinate --	perversely adhering to an opinion, purpose or course in spite of reason -- it is a very effective device to get laughs.
oddity --	nothing results in giggles and belly-laughs than queer, weird behavior.
ogle --	an essential type of physical humor to a comic -- they use their eyes to be amorous, provocative, etc.
opening --	to a comic it's very important to have a good opening to his/her routine -- and naturally the closing is too.

P

Wanda Peepee:

"That Zasu Pitts played the same lovable comic character in so many films. And, let's not forget the wit of Jack Parr. Boy, he could be opinionated and funny at the same time."

THE TOP TEN Ps

pachuco --   a young Mexican-American having a taste for flashy clothes and speaking off-beat words or slang -- often imitated in comedy.

packrat --   another comedy character who loves to hoard all sorts of things to the extreme.

paddle --   a prop often used in comedy -- especially by clowns.

palooka --   an inexperienced boxer -- often used as a comical character.

pansy --   a gay guy -- often used in comedy routines -- usually done to the extreme.

pantomine --   this ancient entertainment is still seen in routines -- very effective -- involves one dancer and a chorus.

party-pooper --   favorite type of comic character putting a sad note on what should be a fun happening-- the response of others results in laughter.

pee --   the need to urinate. Often found in comic scenes -- great for one-liners too.

penquin --   any erect short-legged flightless aquatic bird -- often imitated by comic-- great for physical humor.

pie --   in so many comic shows someone gets a pie pushed in his/her face to the delight of the audience.

Q

Comeé Quicklee:

Comeé Quicklee:

"Most great comics are quick in their delivery and on their feet. If they told a joke that didn't go over, they had to have another to quickly give to the audience."

THE TOP TEN Qs

quack --
making funny noises like "quack, quack," often is used by comics to get laughs.

quadrille --
a square dance for four couples -- often comics use dance in their routines -- doing things in unison is often used.

queery --
a joke often starts out with a why, what, how, where querry.

quandary --
often comical characters take on an exaggerated form of being doughty or a state of perplexity.

quarrelling --
having a dispute about something is a basis of a comical routine.

quaver --
many comic characters cry and will utter their lines in a quaveringly manner -- the whole operation gets plenty of laughs.

queasy --
getting nauseated and then heading to the bathroom is an old routine used in many shows.

queen --
audiences love drag queen bits -- just ask Milton Berle.

queer --
being an exaggerated gay guy results in plenty of laughs.

quicksand --
having a comic character fall into something like quicksand is part of physical comical routines that audiences love.

R

Susan Rubber:

"Tony Randall always gave me a laugh when he played Felix on <u>The Odd Couple</u>.

THE TOP TEN Rs

race --	often used as a setting for a comedy bit -- there is a mad rush to win a contest.
radical --	often a dispute between generations -- <u>All In The Family</u> used it a lot.
radio --	used as a prop to get misinformation -- later TV and cell phones did the same thing-- serves as part of a comedy bit.
ratings --	what keeps a comedian working.
rattle --	toy often used by clowns when they entertain.
razz --	teasing or short for giving someone the co-called raspberry.
rearend --	in adult comedy it refers to kicking someone in the ass.
repartee --	a vital element in good comedy -- the writers give the characters clever, witty or light sparring words to say to each other.
resourceful --	a gift that a stand-up comedian must have (including paying "plants" in audience) to get some laughs.
revenge --	often a device to get the plot moving -- a character wants to get back at someone and comes up with a wild and crazy way to do so.

S

Lucy Suck:

Lucy Suck:

"The Three Stooges -- Curley, Moe, Larry. Now, there was a comic team that gave you plenty of physical humor."

THE TOP TEN Ss

Salome --   a famous character found in the Bible that every commedian loves to imitate -- that includes male comics -- yes the dance of the seven veils has resulted in a lot of laughs.

Satyr --   a combination of a horse/goat man with great sexual attributes -- often found in comic routines in R or X rated "take-offs."

sassy --   being lively, saucy -- often a characteristic assumed by a comic character.

satire --   to ridicule or scorn for laughs -- that's what a lot of stand-ups do.

scalaway --   a southern term meaning scamp -- one who supported the northern intruders -- used a lot in comedies before 1960.

scamp --   an impish, silly person who makes people laugh -- it's what a comic does for a living.

scanty --   a devise used by comedians -- the less clothes and the more impish the facial muscles, the better.

scheme --   thinking up something to solve a problem -- often the central part of a plot in a comedy that goes amiss.

signs --   used a lot -- billboards-- panties -- tattoos to get a laugh.

scintillating --   being witty, lively -- an essential part of any comedians tricks.

T

Joe Tongue:

"If you loved wit, you loved Mark Twain. His observations of humans and their so-called "civilized society" are still being cited today."

THE TOP TEN Ts

tatting -- chatter, gossip -- often a characteristic of a actress in a comedy show.

tattoos -- stand up comics have made all kinds of jokes about them -- sexy meanings, X-rated suggestions, etc.

tease -- a device often used in jest and fun to give an audience a laugh -- it can be simply words along with tickling.

tickle -- to touch the body lightly so as to excite the nerves to cause laughs and giggling.

thinking -- used in comedy -- thinking you are someone else or a thing.

tiptoe -- often used in slapstick comedy -- imitating a ballet dancer -- going toward a thing or person sometimes in unison with others -- very funny if done right.

tomboyish -- a device used by a comedian when becoming or imitating a man -- playing baseball, weight lifting, etc.

toning -- the use of the voice to create a comic effect on the dialogue -- voice goes up and down.

toothy -- often, like Jerry Lewis, a comic with added teeth for a comic affect-- used to make fun of Japanese.

tootsy -- baby talk -- often used to get a laugh -- Fanny Brice who played Babby Snooks and Mollie Sugden on <u>Are You Being Served</u>.

Brabella Unhooked:

"All comics have to be willing to use whatever it takes to make people laugh and let's face it, get a little naughty when necessary."

THE TEN TOP Us

UFO --   so many routines have been made about UFOs and the little people on them -- comics have really used them for plots and scenes.

ugly --   often used in a one-liner -- "Your mama is as ugly as..."---"I'm so ugly..."

unapt --   often comic characters are totally unable to do something -- ride a bike, etc.

unaware --   Gracie Allen did it best -- totally unaware of how dumb she was.

unbeautiful -- most comic characters are ordinary or downright strange looking.

Uncle Tom -- standard funny Negro in many early comedy films- one who smiles and laughs and toes the line -- sometimes played by whites in black face.

unconventional -- found in many comic characters who play people who defy the social standards.

uncouth --   such behavior is found in R or X rated comedies -- farting, belching, etc.

unison --   a very funny comic device -- characters do skipping, walking, etc together -- very funny if done right.

unicyle --   a riding device that is often used by clowns -- they usually ride into something.

V

Vinnie Virgina

"That Dick Van Dyke always could make me smile -- he was so enthusiastic
and yet had an innocence about him."

THE TOP TEN Vs

vaccum -- a prop often used in routines -- to suck up something or someone.

vagabond -- moving from place to place -- a comic must live this kind of life as he learns to go from one gig to another.

vamp -- a seductress -- comediennes love to play this in an extreme way -- males do it in drag.

vanity -- an attitude that says "I'm very special" -- one thinks of Jack Benny.

variety -- often comics appear on variety programs -- like the old Ed Sullivan T.V. show.

vaunt -- to be boastful -- often used in comic sketches and as an aspect of a personality in a comical way.

ventriloquist -- sometimes comics are ventriloquists and make people laugh through their puppets -- one remembers Charlie McCarthy.

vertigo -- a serious medical condition in which one can't keep his/her balance -- used by comics in physical comedy to get laughs.

vehicle -- any moving machine that becomes a setting for a farce -- often the comic will try to drive a bike or something and then drives into someone or something.

venereal -- used in R and X rated one-liners or jokes dealing with love making.

W

Winnie Willey

Winnie Willey

"Give me Johnathan Winters any time. Too bad he never had the chance to team up with Ed Wynn and Mae West. What a comic act they could have dreamed up."

THE TOP TEN Ws

wacky -   acting wild and crazy -- Red Skelton did it best.

wagging --   to move up and down - to and fro - part of comic's storehouse of physical humor devices.

wallop --   part of basic slapskick comedy -- used by clowns a lot -- use paddle or something to kick or hit someone -- aim often for the butt.

weenie --   slang term for penis -- used in non R and X rated shows to entertain the viewers.

weirdo --   strange character but funny -- Monty Python comes to mind -- he and the characters that he works with.

whimsy --   a softer type of comedy -- character is fanciful and naive -- Wally Cox did it best.

whoop-de-do --   a loud yell of jubilation -- can be in the form of a hoot.

wiggling --   move to and fro -- part of physical comedy.

willy --   another slang term for penis -- not R or X rated- but still very effective to those wanting adult humor.

wordplay --   very sophisticated type of comedy -- not only includes puns but changing words -- saying them in unison -- comics on Third Rock From the Sun do it very well.

X

Boner X-rated:

"Can't think of any comic whose name starts with X. So, let's list other great female comediennes: Penny Marshall, Phyllis Diller, Gracie Allen, Betty White Roseanne, Dawn French, Carol Burnett, Fany Brice, Eve Arden, Kay Ballard, Estelle Getty, Rue McClanahan and Bea Arthur."

THE TOP TEN Xs

X -- often used by comics and others to indicate the unknown (gender, element, etc.) that leads to a punch line that identifys the X -- also indicate dirty humor - adults only.

x-ray -- often used by comics telling jokes about doctors -- sometimes used as a prop.

X-rated -- this material is only for adults -- deals with really dirty sexual matters.

Xmas -- refers to jokes about anything dealing with the Christmas season -- Santa, reindeer, etc.

Xhosa -- comics use the Bantu dialect when telling funny jokes about this African tribe --or any African tribe -- dialects make the jokes funnier.

X-radiation -- again used by comics telling hospital/doctor jokes.

X-chromosome -- often referred to by comics who like to tell XXX rated sex jokes.

Xer -- a member of Generation X who have an off-beat zany sense of humor.

xerophile -- used by comics who love to tell jokes about people who fear all foreigners.

Xanadu -- when comics tell jokes about wonderful, exotic places, they often call them Xanadu.

Y

Hank Yank:

Hank Yank:

"Let's take our hats off to Alan Young. He was so funny and so willing to be upstaged by Mr. Ed -- a horse."

THE TOP TEN Ys

yahoo -- a yell to get someone's attention -- often used in an exaggerated way by comics.

yakking -- to talk, chatter persistently -- often a aspect of a comic character.

yikes -- an expression of astonishment -- again often exaggerated by comics.

yokel -- a gullible person -- again often found in comic characters.

yoo-hoo -- a friendly way to get someone's attention -- incorporated into some comic characters.

yo-yo -- a stupid or foolish person -- target of jokes.

yoyoing -- to fluctuate -- part of stapslick.

yummy -- to a comic it is used in an exaggerated way to express pleasure.

YMCA -- often the scene of a comedy sketch --often with gay characters.

you-all -- a Southern expression that is incorporated in a comic character playing a Southern person -- Blanche on The Golden Girls.

Z

Frits Zipper:

"Can't think of any comic whose name starts with Z. So, let's list other male comics who were great: Harvey Korman, Flip Wilson Mel Brooks, Bud Abbot and Lou Costello, Art Carney Jerry Lewis and Stan Lauel and Oliver Hardy."

THE TOP TEN Zs

zany --	a subordinate clown or acrobat in old comedies who mimics the tricks of the principal.
zero --	Mostel -- the comic actor who made so many laugh.
zig-zag --	part of physical comedy -- you go this way and then that way.
zipper --	often used in R-rated comedy bits about the guy's fly being open.
zippy --	very fast and quick -- essential element for many funny routines to work well.
zoo --	often the setting for a comic bit.
zooks --	used as a mild oath -- part of an old comic's routine in vaudeville.
zoot suit --	a suit of extreme cut -- popular during the 1940s especially among Blacks -- now used in comic bits about the 40s.
zooty --	flashing in manner of style -- in dress, dance -- often used for comic effect.
Zulu --	a member of the Bantu tribe -- comics used to blacken their faces and pretend to be tribal members who would dance and tell African ethnic jokes.

Poems About Buddy Alley's Love Life

Angela

I was sad and
    looking for love
when I went by a
    gospel tent.

From the tent
    I heard a beautiful
voice saying:
    "Repent, come in
and be in the light."

I was so desperate
    for love that
I went in and
    saw Sister Angela.

She was like
    an angel from Heaven.
She was at the altar
    dressed in a white robe

with the Cross of Jesus
    resting on her full
bosom.

Angela was a
    true beauty.
The spot light
    above her
seemed like a heavenly
    beam to
embrace Angela with God's
    protective
arms around her.

As she preached,
    I noticed her blue eyes,
lovely blonde hair,
    full lips and
inviting smile.

The chorus behind her
    sang hymns of
praise to the Lord.
    Often, you
heard shouts of
    "Hallelujah,
Hallelujah, Hallelujah!"

Since I was desperate
    for love,

I went up to the
    altar and embraced
not only the Lord but
    Sister Angela.

Making love to Angela
    was like going
to Heaven to receive
    a kiss and a blow job
from the Lord.

We went through a
    ritual before
Sister Angela and I
    made love.

We knelt and prayed
    for mutual orgasm.
We undressed and with heavenly
    sounds from a CD
enjoyed the 69th movement.

Then I mounted her
    like a vessel
from the Lord.
    I thrust my cock into
Angela -- gently at first
-- then faster.

Making love to Angela
    was like playing

a song of praise on the harp
    to the Lord.

When we reached orgasm,
    we shouted,
"Hallelujah! Hallelujah!"
    After that,
"Amen! Amen! Amen!

Angel loved to have us
    play great lovers
from the Bible:
    Rachel and Jacob
    Delilah and Samson
    Ruth and Boaz.

Then, it all ended.
    Into the gospel
tent walked a stud from
    Brazil.

His name was Columbo
    and he had
that Latin American look
    that is as
sexy as hell.

Besides having a
    warm smile,
he had strong arms
    and thighs.

Angela loved him
    at first sight.
And when he took
    his clothes off
to be baptized,
    she lit up
like a neon sign.

As he rose from
    the lake,
he revealed a cock
    that was
9 inches long.

I knew I was a
    goner when
Angela shouted,
    "Hallelujah!
Hallelujah! Praise
    The Lord."

Yes, at that moment
    I decided
to leave Angela.
    Even Moses
would have had a hard time
    competing
with what I saw.

Yes, Columbo's dick and
    balls swung

like a bunch of bananas
    at the market.

So, I left and
    continued my
journey to find love.
    I knew I could never
compete with the noble and hung
    Montezuma

COCA

I went to the library
    looking for a sexy DVD
and came away with a hot
    librarian named Coca.

Coca looked so plain
    with her glasses and her red
hair done up in a bun
    with a gold clip.

Yet underneath lay
    an imprisoned spirit of
a sexy volcano ready
    to explode.

We hit it off
    right away.
We had read a lot
    of the same books.

Yes, we shared a passion
    for the works of
Tennessee Williams,
    Somerset Maugham
and D.H. Lawrence.

In the semi-darkness of
    her bedroom I
found that underneath
    Coca's conservative

outward persona lay an
    unbridled passion.

As I road her I found
    that I experienced
sexual ecstasy
    beyond my wildest dreams.

Yes, her full bosom and
    round firm ass
along with her red-haired
    pussy excited me
and hardened my dong.

Coca loved for us
    to play the great
lovers of literature
    and history.

She would be Cleopatra
    to my Anthony
She would be Josephine
    to my Napoleon.
She would be Scarlet
    to my Rhett.

Yes, Coca was
    hot, hot, hot.
But, she had one
    hangup that
made me fearful.

What you ask?
    Well, it was that
she enjoyed making
    love in an
atmosphere of danger.

I know what you are thinking,
    "Buddy, you didn't give
Coca up just for that. Buddy,
    you had it all baby.
Coca was like a bowl of cherries
    with whipped cream."

Sorry, dear reader. I had to
    give up Coca.
You see, she liked making love in
    the stacks where someone
might see us.

Even worse, she liked getting
    naked and doing it on
a book cart.
    Once as we were rocking
back and forth, the cart
    started rolling.

Several times I told Coca,
    "We must stop this. It is
too dangerous."
    She replied, "Buddy baby
enjoy the danger -- it makes our sex hotter."

Buddy Alley

Well, one day her boss
    stopped us and
showed us a video of
    what we had been
doing.

Yes, the surveillance
    camera had
captured it all. There
    was Buddy's hard
dong and swinging balls
    humping Coca.

So, I had to move on.
    Buddy loves danger
but he doesn't want to
    get arrested.

Yes, despite my passion
    for Coca's red-haired
hole of creation, I
    dropped her like a
hot potato.

By the way, Coca wasn't
    fired.
You see, her boss
    had once been on
the book cart.

INDIRA

Once I was so
    desperate for love
that I sought out
    advice from a
fortune teller.

Her name was Joyce
    but she called herself
"Princess Indira"
    for business purposes.

She claimed she
    came from India
and had gained her
    powers from Vishnu.

She was an
    exotic woman to me
with her gold turban
    and long
flowing golden silk robe.

After I told her
    my quest for love,
she looked into her crystal ball
    and whispered,
"Ah, I see her in my
    crystal ball."

"Who is she, who is she?"
    I asked.
Then she took my hand and
    gently guided it
to her voluptuous breast
    and whispered,
"It is I -- Indira."

Being in love with Indira
    was exciting.
She used her crystal ball
    and the ouija boards
to discover how we should
    make love.

There for awhile
    the ball and the
ouija boards told us to
    make love in all
the ways I really enjoy.

Yes, we did it front,
    back, sideways and
upside down.
    It was wonderful
and so exciting making
    love with Indira.

Then, one day, Indira said
    that the signs

demanded that I be tied
    to the bedpost,
whipped and gagged as
    she road me
"cowgirl" style.

After several sessions
    I felt like a
road under construction.
    My arms, butt and
balls ached from the
    experience.

So, I had to end
    my affair with
"Princess Indira."
    I had lost faith
in the crystal ball
    and the ouija
boards.

My balls, dick and butt
    ached for weeks
after I left Indira.
    But, I was happy
I had left her.
    I felt like I had
survived the sinking of
    the Titanic.

JUDY

When I went to
    the races,
I fell in love
    with Judy.

It was love
    at first sight.
She was bending
    over looking at
her engine.

She was dressed in
    an orange outfit.
When I saw her,
    the only thing I could
think was,
    "What an ass!"

You see, dear reader,
    I'm an ass man.
I love making love from
    the rear end position.

I can't explain it,
    but I just go crazy
when I see a small hard ass.
    Must be the
primeval animal in me.

Then, when Judy stood up,
    I got a heart on --
as hard as a rock.
    You see, she had a
full bosom and an 18" waist
    and blonde hair.

At the track they
    nicknamed her
"Jumping Judy" because
    she drove so fast.

I introduced myself
    and our romance
took off like a
    rocket to the moon.

Judy liked to drive up
    mountain roads.
I was there next to her,
    with my crash helmet.

Once in awhile
    she would stop
and park so we could
    make love.

During the love making
    she would use her foot
to gun up the engine
    between orgasms.

Buddy Alley

Wow, what a fantastic
    time we had.
I should have purchased a
    small crash helmet
for my dick. Why?
    Because Judy drove up
those mountain roads so fast.

I was going to propose
    to Judy
but another race track driver --
    Heinrich from Germany ---
came along.

Same old story,
    the stud had a longer
-- and in this case — faster
    rocket than I.
So, I had to move on.

Thought about surgery
    to extend my 7" cock
to a 9" but I gave it up. Why?

    Too expensive and besides
I still needed to increase
    my speed.

NICKOLAS

I met a dancer
    named Nickolas
who had fled Russia
    to come to America.

He was a ballet
    dancer who
was as strong
    as an ox.

Yes, his arms
    and thighs
were well-developed.
    He had no
problem lifting a
    ballerina.

Besides that
    he had a peter
that was so long that when stiff,
    it reached his navel.

Unfortunately for me
    he took a
passionate liking
    for me.

You see, Nicholas
    was as gay

Buddy Alley

as a humming bird
    in spring.

And dear reader,
    when I say gay I
don't mean happy
    but queer as
a queen bee.

Backstage he would
    approach me
from the rear
    I often felt his
strong fingers gliding
    up and down
the crack in my butt.

I told him
    many, many times,
"No, no Nicholas
    I'm not gay."

He only smiled
    with an impish grin
and whispered,
    "Now Buddy,
don't be coy with me.
    You are gay
and a virgin too."

Once, he trapped me
    in the alley outside
the theatre.
    He threw me
against the brick wall
    unzipped my fly and
reached into my pants to have his
    way with me.

I was only saved by
    other cast members
from being de-flowered
    right there
in the alley.

Well, I'll admit
    that I finally gave in.
Yes, back stage I let him
    pull down my pants
-- and yes my Calvin Kleins.
He shoved his cock
    up my ass.

I found the act
    wonderful.
You see, Nicholas had
    come well prepared.
He knew that K-Y would
    give me a gentle ride.

Buddy Alley

Wow, this guy knew the
    positions for the game.
He headed his penis to the
    right to hit
the G spot.

He even kissed me on the
    neck and lips
as he road me until both of
    us exploded in a
mutual orgasm.

But once he had
    had me,
he never came back.
    I was just
another piece of meat to him.

What really got me mad
    is that he told
others, "I've had Buddy
    -- good lay but
(get this) his alley is
    too wide. I
need a tight ass to
    end my dance."

TITANIUM

Titanium was a scientist
    who worked in a lab.
Her father had been a
    a professor of chemistry
and named all his children after
    elements on the lab chart.

While she wore glasses,
    she still was attractive
because of her long blonde hair,
    blue eyes, full bosom
and hard behind.

She took a liking to me
    because I was in the
academic world too.
    While she taught me more
about science,
    I taught her more about
world history.

Love with her was
    quite different if
not down right clinical.
    You see, she loved to
measure my cock and balls
    before and while I got
an erection.

Naturally, she took my
    blood pressure readings.
After the love session she
    always collected my
cum and then took new measurements
    and blood pressure readings.

At first I didn't know what to
    make of it all.
But, I needed love -- and sexual release --
    so I went along.

We always reached climax --
    mutual orgasm was very common.
Why? because she knew every move to
    bring it about.
She prided herself on being an
    expert on G-Spots.

Then, one day I found at least
    50 log books ---
each contained detailed data
    on one of the males
she had had an affair with.

I felt like a lab rat.
    Titanium wasn't in love
with me. Oh no.
    She was collecting data

to write a book on the
        sexual behavior of the
American male.

So, one day during one of our
        "experiments", I put
my Calvin Kleins back on and
        walked out on
Titanium.

As I walked out of the lab,
        I thought to myself,
"I may need ass along with a
        hot orgasm but I'm not
going to be a rat to get them."

ZOLA

I fell in
    love
with a circus
    performer
by the name of
    Zola.

She came from
    Nigeria
and was as
    beautiful
as Africa --
    dark, mysterious
and exciting.

She had an act
    that featured
monkeys.
She used bananas
    as rewards
for their tricks.

When she appeared
    in the center ring
she was dressed
    in bananas.

Yes, her bra
    was made of bananas.

Her g-string was
    composed of
bananas.

Her monkeys
    would do
anything for
    bananas.

They would swing
    on the trapeze.
They would leap
    from one place
to another for
    bananas.

Zola's finale
    was fantastic.
She would look up
    at the monkeys
and yell, "Come and
    get them."

The monkeys would then
    leap down
to get the bananas
    that composed
Zola's costume.

After they undressed
    Zola,

they would all line-up
    and bow.

As Zola stood naked
    before the world,
the audience went wild
    for Zola.

Her voluptuous
    breasts, legs
and ass
    created a
gorgeous image of
    Mother Africa.

Members of the
    audience
took photos of Zola
    and her
cute monkeys.

To make love
    to Zola was
an adventure into
    the dark
world of Africa.

One entered her
    and felt
surrounded by
    black velvet.

When I came,
    it was like a
volcano erupting --
    shooting its hot lava
into the Bush.

Oh, how I loved
    Zola.
But, I wasn't
    enough.
No, she bought
    a 9-inch black
vibrator and left
    for her next gig
with her monkeys.

Yes, I learned that
    Zola only
found true love in
    the arms of
a man from Africa.

MEET TWO CLOWNS

GEORGE BENNY AND GRACIE BENNY

AND SOME OF THEIR STUDENTS
WHO CAUGHT "CLOWNITIS"

FROM THEM

George and Gracie Benny are both teachers at a high school. George teaches social studies while Gracie teaches German.

Both are well educated. George has a B.A. and an M.A. in history. And Gracie has a B.A. and a M.A. in German. They have taken a lot of courses over and above their M.A.s

While they are very devoted to teaching their chosen field of expertise, they like to put a lot of humor into their teaching.

When they met each other at the University of Illinois, they discovered that beneath their serious personas were imps. This lead to a lot of fun sex and laughs. After they married they continued to be imps. They enjoyed one-liners, jokes, pranks and yes raunchy humor.

It has taken courage for them to show their impish behavior. Teacher evaluations and viewing and listening devices have made it difficult at times to engage in pranks and fun.

However, both have continued to enjoy clownish behavior. They love to dress up in costumes. Such things brightens up their teaching days. Also, their clownish approach to life has spread happiness to their students and colleagues.

In the following pages you will see Gracie and George being imps.

So, Gracie who are you supposed to be?

Well, I'm dressed as the Queen of Hearts for Valentine's Day

Why?

Well, when I teach German today I'm giving every student a card for Valentine's Day. Naturally the greeting "I love you" will be written in German. I'll also pass out some chocolate candy that will have the shape of a heart.

Then, in German I will tell them about some of the great love stories of different couples in plays and in history.

Can you think of any funny TV show that featured valentines?

Yes, on one episode of <u>The Golden Girls</u> the gals go off for a week to a hotel that they later find out is a nudish camp. But, they decide to join in and take off their clothes and go down to dinner using large valentines to cover themselves up.

Hi George.

So, what are you up to? Why the lederhosen?

Well, my wife teaches German and she wanted me to do a comic routine with her in her German class. We plan to do some traditional German folk dances.

I see. Where did you get the idea? From some comic show?

Yes, it was <u>Are You Being Served</u>. They had one show entitled "German Week."
So, what is the routine?

My wife - Frau Webb - and I will sing German songs, drink a toast to the students and then dance a polka.

Good luck. Hope you get some laughs.

What are you doing?

I am taking a bath.

I can see that. But, why are you holding the wash cloth over your face?

I'm playing peepaboo. I'm trying to get my hubby to be naughty, if you know what I mean.

I understand. Good luck! What is your favorite scene on a TV comedy show?

That's easy! It is the Greek wedding scene on <u>Are You Being Served</u>. Mr. Humphries and Mrs. Slocombe are so funny as they and other cast members dance at the wedding.

Why are you dressed that way?

I like to dress like Sherlock Holmes when I give my students in history a historical problem to solve. It makes it more fun.

What scene in a TV comedy show gave you the most laughs?

The show where Dorothy Zbornak and her mother Sophia Petrillo sing like Sonny Bono and Cher. It was a hoot! I loved <u>The Golden Girls</u>.

Well, what happened to you?

I'm fine. I'm pretending to be in critical condition as a result of the Cubs losing to the Cardinals. I'm a big Cub fan and I have a lot of friends who are Cardinal fans. They love to tease me about the Cubs.

Well, I must say, you look pitiful.

Thanks, that's how wish to look.

Where did you get the idea?

From comedy shows. Practically all of them use the device of being injured. And, it works. It results in a lot of laughs.

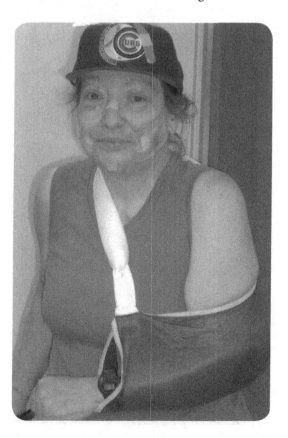

Well Gracie, what are you up to now?

I'm dressed like a rabbit.

Why?

Well, Easter will be here soon so I thought I would be the Easter Bunny. I'll tell my students in German all about the Easter Bunny and then pass out eggs and candy.

Sounds like fun.

I hope so.

Can you think of any show that featured the Easter Bunny.

Sure can. On <u>The</u> <u>Vicar</u> all the main characters dress up like rabbits after Mrs. Cropley dies. Before she passed on she ask anyone who came to see her to do the job of dressing up like a Easter Bunny. So, they all do it -- much to the surprise of them all.

I see that you like clowns.

Oh, yes indeed in fact I was a clown for a short time in the Shriners

What comic show do you like to remember the most?

Well, there are so many. But, when it comes to clowns, I love to remember the show where Dick Van Dyke appears on <u>The</u> <u>Golden</u> <u>Girls</u>. He plays a lawyer who wants to give up law and become a clown. He appears as a clown to defend one of the golden girls. That show was so funny. He had a very large red nose and hugh shoes. It was made all the more funny because he was doing the clown bit in a court room.

Are you two getting ready for Christmas?

Yes we are.

Do you have a favorite funny Christmas show?

We both agree on two shows that were filled with belly-laughs.

One was on <u>The Vicar</u>. The new vicar is invited to too many Christmas dinners and she has to take a tractor home.

The other was on Fraiser. Fraiser pretends to be Jewish to impress his girl friend's mother. But, in the middle of doing this, in walks Neils dressed as Jesus Christ.

What are you up to with that umbrella?

I'm at the Fine Arts Festival. I'm pretending to be a male Mary Poppins.

I see. Well, good luck on flying. What is your favorite comedy scene?

It was on <u>Frasier</u>. Niles and Frasier have opened up a new restaurant. They put too much liqueur in the cherry-jubilee so when Roz lights it, it explodes all over her. Every time I see it I nearly laugh my "balls" off.

Well, we meet you again. So elfy what are you up to?

I am showing off some of the many costumes that I wear to teach German.

The first is Black Peter who helps St. Nickolas in Germany. He brings gifts to all the bad kids.

The second is a Pilgrim lady. And, of course, the last is Mrs. Claus.

Why do you like doing the costume bit?

Well, it helps teach German and it gives me an identify. They call me "Frau Costume Lady."

What comedy show do you enjoy remembering?

I enjoyed so many of the I Love Lucy shows. She loved dressing up in costumes too. My favorite is when she is a bull and Desi is a bull fighter. It was hilarious. The bull makes eyes at Desi and dances around the ring.

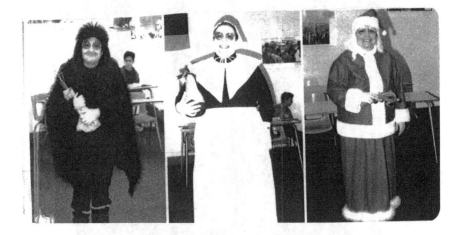

WOW GRACIE, YOU HAVE OUTFITS
TO PLAY CLEOPATRA, BRUNNHIDA
AND MARLENE DIETRICH

You are truly the
IMP OF THE YEAR

CLEOPATRA

BRUNNHILDE

Louise as Marlene Dietrich
"Falling in Love Again"

MEET OUR STUDENTS

INTERVIEWING TWO ELFS*

What are you two up to?

Trying to get some laughs. People will see us and think we are using the same bathroom.

I guess so.

Also, it looks like two people are spying on others. You find that in so many comedy shows.

You're so right. Characters overhear something, get things totally wrong and it leads to all sorts of funny things.

That's right. You find it in <u>Fraiser</u>, <u>Third Rock from the Sun</u>, <u>I Love Lucy</u> and so many others.

---

* Students agreed to do these gag shots for fun.

INTERVIEW WITH TWO IMPS

What are you up two? Did the gal just win?

No! We are just playing -- fooling around.

What do you mean?

Well, in so many comedy shows there is the battle of the sexes -- men vs. women.

So true -- it's a favorite device in comedy. What are some of your favorite couples who fight?

We all love Lucy fighting with Desi. And then there is Frasier versus his ex.

INTERVIEW WITH TWO CLOWNS

Why are you using that paddle like that?

To get laughs that's why.

Where did you get the idea?

From clowns that perform at circuses. They love to chase each other around the ring swinging a bat or a paddle or something like that.

Well, you certainly look like to mean it.

Great! That's the idea.

INTERVIEW WITH A CLOWN

Girl, what have you been up to?

Well, I have been up to a lot of pranks.

I can see that. So, what is your favorite comedy scene in a TV show?

I loved to watch <u>Frasier</u>. There were so many cute episodes. One of the best was when Niles and Frasier go to an exclusive spa. They find themselves wrapped in warm blankets from neck to toes and then find themselves being surrounded by bees. It was hilarious.

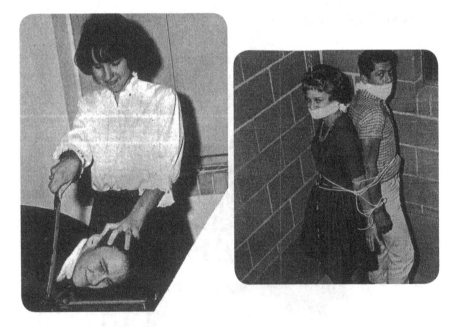

FUN BONUSES

An Ode To Michael Lucas

Oh how I adore to look
upon your outward persona.
Ah, so handsome, so attractive,
so styishly tailored.

But, I see Michael underneath
your public persona an
Imp that is ready for some
fun and mischief.

That imp can't hide from me,
I see it in your eyes,
yes, and in your mischievous
smile and gestures.

What, you say, that isn't true
that you are only striving
to present a man's passion
for the attributes of the male
body ---
a long and wide cock,
an bubble-like and firm ass,
large, dangling testicles,
and a kissable asshole.

Well, Michael I agree to that,
and you do it with style and class.
Yes, you do it in different ways to meet
the needs of your clientele.

Buddy Alley

Some want tenderness and romance
in their love making.
Others want toughness and adventure
in showing their love.

But, Michael, don't you have a lot of
impish fun doing both?
Don't you become Fellini-like in putting
together your great productions?

Look at the locations that you give the
actors to make love:
beaches, speed boats, kitchens,
caves, candle lit rooms.
--- and even staircases,

Now Michael these all lend themselves
to funny positions and clownlike behavior.
In fact one must be an acrobate in order
to make love -- up against a wall,
upside down, etc. etc.
I don't need to list anymore, Michael
you can fill in the rest.

Some of your actors are trained
in dance and it is a good thing
because you require them to leap
and jump as they make love.

You love to have your actors
in motion -- running along beaches,

going to Coney Island, skipping, etc.
They are often smiling and ready
for impish love games.

You have lots of impish fun
I'm sure planning sexual play
with two or more clowns at love games.
Some of the positions often show
two or three sets of balls and cocks
at play stacked on top of each other.

Yes, I have laughed my "balls" off
at some of the positions that you have arranged.
I often wondered how the actors could keep
from laughing at where they found themselves.

But, most go along with it,
and they "ah" and "oh" and say
"give it to me hard baby" and
other things that go with
the impish scene:

shaking butt-cheeks
kissing buttholes
licking balls and cocks,
riming assholes
and sucking heads.

I must hand it to the jesters,
they do the scenes with tenderness.
Once in a great while, one finds

a clownish smile or giggle
coming from a participant.

So, how did I find you out?
Well, you made a film entitled,
Michael Lucas' <u>La Dolce Vita</u>.
That's when I realized you
admired the work of Fellini.
And Fellini loved to poke
fun at society.

Then in one of your <u>Collections</u>
you were having sex with two other guys
in all sorts of ways but with
tenderness. But, then I noticed the draps--
they had a diamond pattern and the
diamonds were pink and black and I remembered the
jesters who entertained courts
during the middle ages.
I thought to myself, "That rascal! He is being
a clown!"

Yes, Michael Lucas,
under that persona
is a clown -- a jester.

But, we love you for it --
so amusing, so creative, so
Fellini-like.

And to capture all
the sexual fun,
you hire the best in
in show biz.

Talk about exciting
choreography!
Talk about creative
camera work!
Talk about a great
sound crew!

May God give you a long
good life so that you may
continue to please us with
your impish ways of
looking at funny things that
people do.

What, you say I'm wrong.
But, who but an imp
would have every love
guy on the bottom getting
"love juice" sprayed
in his face and then invited
to suck his lover's creamy
LOLLYPOP?

No, Michael you are
the Fellini of gay porn
with the creative spirits of
Pagliaccio and Romeo.

BUDDY ALLEY IN DRAG

For years as part of my act I would dress up as Mae West, Marilyn Monroe, Marlene Dietrich and Cher. Once in awhile I did it for charity. I became a bride to help raise money for the Comic Relief Foundation. Here is an account of the event which was held on June 20, 1954. It was held at the Al Jolson Chapter of the Comic Relief Foundation in Chicago.

I WAS A BRIDE FOR A DAY

Here I am (Gloria Cheesecake) and my mother (the Comedienne Dixie Allen).

120

"Here comes the bride, all dressed in white."

That's what the organist started to play as I was standing in my long flowing bridal gown getting ready to gracefully march into the Chapter room that was packed with people. I was the star attraction in the last act in the Chapter's tongue-in-cheek fashion show.

I looked gorgeous, if I do say so.

My white wedding dress was made of taffeta and featured a narrow waist, a full skirt and a plunging neckline. Long white gloves up to my elbows added to my vision of elegance.

Underneath my gown I was wearing a jockstrap and a long-line bra that not only helped elevate my "falsies" but pushed in my gut. By the way, for boobies I used white balloons that had been filled with water. They gave me a very full bosom. I thought to myself, "Stand aside Jane Russell. Here I come, girl." To make the skirt fuller I wore a interlining made of crinoline. I also had on white nylon stockings that went up to my groin. My feet were in a pair of white high heels. As I stood there, trying to get my breath and balance myself, I though, "I hope that I can pull this off."

My long, curly lush burnette hair added to my glamorous appearance. It, of course, was a wig that Betty, one of the ladies in the bridal party, had found among her things. She said that it dated from her "wild Sophia Loren period."

To set off the outfit I wore a small crown made of pearls and a long veil made of Chantilly lace. Besides complimenting the wedding dress, it helped to hide my identify and achieve the illusion that I was a young bride.

To make me even more gorgeous Betty did my make up. A light tan foundation by Maybelline was applied to my face to cover up any hint of a beard and then a little rouge was applied to my cheeks. To highlight my naturally beautiful dark brown eyes, long eyelashed and eye shadow were applied. For my lips Betty had selected "passion pink" made by Avon. Some of Liz Taylor's White Diamonds perfume was put behind my ears to give me an alluring romantic fragrance.

My bridesmaids, bless them, also gave me something old, something borrowed and something blue. The something old was a pearl necklace, the something blue was a garter, and the something borrowed was an engagement ring. Then, the dears, presented me with a large bridal bouque of white and pink carnations. When I looked in the mirror, I saw an image of loveliness. I thought, "Why do they need Dame Edna when they can have me."

Well, as the organist continued to play Wagner's "Wedding March," the siding door which separates the anteroom from the Chapter room was opened and the wedding party started slowly making its way up front to the altar where the minister and bridegroom were anxiously waiting. As a new bride, I should have felt nervous but I didn't. I only thought, "Gosh, this is a great put-on."

"Here comes the bride, all dressed in white."

My four bridesmaids -- all in pink -- went in first, followed by two flowergirls who threw flower pedals to cover my pathway. I slowly started my walk to the altar. I decided to give them the old Mae West walk--hips swaying, butt gyrating. My boobies, thanks to the water-filled balloons shook like jello. I blew kisses to the audience. They loved it. I was really knocking them dead. I heard someone whisper, "Who is it anyway?" Somebody else replied, "I don't know, but look at those boobies. Wow!"

On hearing that comment, I couldn't resist stopping, raising my skirt to reveal my blue garter. Several guys in the audience whistled. I couldn't help thinking to myself, "Nicole Kidman eat your heart out!"

The bridal party finally reached the altar where the minister stood in a clerical robe with the bridegroom. He/She (actually Comedienne Debbie More) funny with his/her tuxedo, rabbit ears, buck teeth, large thick lensed eyeglasses, and a large fuzzy bunny tail. He/She was eating a carrot.

Then, I heard the minister say, "Dearly beloved, we are here today to celebrate the coming together of Gloria Cheesecake with Peter Rabbit. If there is anyone here who knows of any reason why these two should not be joined together in holy matrimony, let them speak now or forever be silent." On cue all the bridesmaids raised their hands -- however, nobody said anything. Members of the audience only giggled.

Then, the minister looked at me and asked, "Do you, Gloria take Peter as your lawfully wedded husband -- to honor and obey . . .?" You know the rest. I replied in a high pitched voice, "I do--do --do!"

"Do you Peter take Gloria as your lawfully wedded wife -- to honor and obey . . .?"

Peter stopped chewing his carrot and replied, "That's right Doc!"

"You may kiss the bride."

Peter raised my veil and kissed me on the cheek much to the surprise of the audience. Some were in shock by this time. Others were really into the fantasy. I heard someone yell out, "Aren't they special!"

Then, as the organist began to play Mendelsohn's "Bridal March," Peter and I turned around and looked at the audience. I threw my bouquet into the crowd. It was caught by a startled Ruth Hiss, age 77. She exclaimed, "Oh my Lord, I'm not ready for this!" The audience laughed with delight. At that point the entire wedding party marched through the Chapter room and to the anteroom.

A wedding reception was held downstairs in the dining room. Dainty sandwiches were served along with punch and wedding cake. All in all the fashion show was a very good fund raiser. After paying for expenses, we made a profit of about $500.00.

Of course, everyone thought that the wedding at the end -- and especially the young bride -- was the hit of the entire show. By the way, for those of you who really got into the fantasy, the site of the honeymoon was somewhere in the Virgin Islands.

RISQUE JOKES FOR ELVES, IMPS AND CLOWNS

A

How did Eve try to hide the forbidden apple from Adams?

By putting it between her cheeks in her butt. She didn't have a bra until much later.

B

How did Ed water the flowers without a hose?

He pissed on them to empty his bladder.

C

Why did Lola and her lover Roger have to call 911?

Roger accidentally grabbed Elmer's Glue rather than the K-Y.

D

Why did Lenny have an aching asshole?

He had been double-headed.

E

Why couldn't Marty ejaculate?

Fred's ass wasn't tight enough.

F

Why didn't Gloria have any laughs during sex with her lover Bob?

She couldn't read the comic strips with the lights off.

G

When my sexy lover asked me if that "was a gun" in my pants or if "I was just glad" to see her, I replied the following:

"Well now it's just glad to see you. Your sexy look was so powerful that my gun went off."

H

Why did Hilda divorce her lesbian lover Victoria?

Because she insisted on wearing her hiking boots and tool belt when she was having sex.

I

Why didn't Betty like Ken, the soda jerk, to make a banana split for her?

Because he arranged the banana and scoopes of icecream in an obscene way with whipped cream and a cherry on top.

Why did Japanese "ladies of pleasure" bow a lot?

To practice getting their heads in the right place to please their male customers.

K

Why did Rose find herself without a boyfriend after several hot sessions of love making?

Because she was accused of kissing and then telling everyone that his dicks was only two inches long.

L

What's true of most men's love-handles?

They contain 80 percent of their brains.

M

What gives men an instant fantasy that they are 18 again?

One tablet of viagra which is placed under the tongue -- and 25 minutes for it to dissolve.

N

How did Bud get Louise to take off her nightie for some hot love play?

Using his tongue on her nipples and G -spots.

O

Why is a gay man's tongue so important?

Its used to arouse passion and to open the back door of the tunnel of love.

P

Why shouldn't a woman judge a man by the size of his nose or foot?

Because they have nothing to do with the size of his penis.

Q

What do you mean by a "quicky?"

It means that the sex session lasted 29 seconds. (20 seconds for penetration and 4 seconds of ejaculation)

R

Why do most women dislike their husbands when they insist on "riding to climax" on top of them?

When the guy's weigh is over 200 and can't reach orgasm fast enough.

S

How did gay Ted make his lover happy during sex play?

He let him straddle his face so he could enjoy Ted's sucking and riming abilities.

T

True or False. The more cum a gay guy ejaculates indicates the more he has enjoyed the love making with his lover?

Answer. Very definitely

U

What is so unique about Australia?

When it comes to sex, the phrase "down under" takes on an entirely different meaning.

V

In the military what does the letters VD stand for?

Victory and Defense against members of the armed services getting any one of the so-called "veneral diseases."

W

What four Ws are vital to having wild sex?

weenie

willy

waggling

walloping

When a film is rated XXX, what does it mean to anyone under 18?

"I've got to see it."

What was Eldon John's favorite song?

Y.M.C.A.

When a guy sees that another man's zipper is open what should he say?

Use a variation of a Mae West response: "Did you just pee or do you want me to shake hands with your door knob?"

X

When a film is rated XXX, what does it mean to anyone under 18?

"I've got to see it."

Y

What is Elton John's favorite song?

"Y.M.C.A"

Z

When a gal sees that a man's pants zipper is open, what should she say?

Use a variation of a Mae West response: "Did you just pee or do you want me to turn your "door knob" and warm up your balls.

A DITTY ABOUT HOW TO HAVE FUN SEX

BY BUDDY ALLEY

Nothing like fun sex
    to feel terrific.
After orgasm you feel like
    you have had the 4th of July
along with Christmas.

    Giggle, Giggle, Giggle

The best way to get it
    is the marry another clown.
Don't go by his/her outward
    appearance.
Oh no -- the rule should be:
    "If he/she isn't ticklish and can't
giggle, drop him / her fast.

    Ha, Ha, Ha

Clowns who have fun sex
    know where all the
G-spots are and have

developed their kissing,
sucking, riming and fingering
skills.

Ho, Ho, Ho

They know were to go to get
ideas to put fun into sex.
Yes, they love to shop at Patricia's
to get toys, costumes,
rubbers and lotions to enhance
orgasm.

Giggle, Gigggle, Giggle

They also love to see
porno films together to
get some new ideas. So many are
a hoot.

Yes, nothing like a
New Sensation or Lucas DVD to
give clowns ideas to provide variety
in terms of their love-play.
Talk about settings and
positions!

Ha, Ha, Ha

Yes, clowns learn that they can
make love in barns, on beaches,
in trees, in swimming pools, in

cars, on balconies and even
on kitches tables, stoves, and
    sinks.

Wow, Wow, Wow

And, they can see from the
    videos that they can do it
lying down, sideways and even
    upside down.

Chuckle, Chuckle, Chuckle

Clowns also make sure that
    they communicate
during and after sex.
    They love to make sounds
during hot sessions. What kind?
    These: "ahs, ohs" are
uttered along with "yes, yes,
    give it to me baby."

Hot, Hot, Hot

Afterwards, they relate what
    gave them the most pleasure.
This leds to another hot session
    or at least makes them look
forward to their next encounter.

Oh Baby! Oh Baby! Oh Baby!

AN X RATED TAKE ON HIGH-TECH DEVICES AND FADS

How a dirty comic might look at the new high-tech devices:

X

RATED

IPHONE

Twitter -- sounds during sex play

Pandora -- forbidden actions

Apple Store -- where Eve met Adam

Google -- ways to leer in a sexy manner

Facebook -- pictures of nude people wanting to get together

Internet -- a device used by nude couples or groups to swing together

Numbers -- phone numbers of those seeking connections

Extras -- props available to enjoy sex so each reaches climax -- also containers to keep cum and to store rubbers -- used and unused

Comics are having a ball with symbolic visuals that might be referred to as logos. Here are a few:

R

RIPS IN JEANS

1. RIP OVER RIGHT KNEE __ I'm straight and hot.

2. RIP OVER LEFT KNEE __ I'm gay and hot.

3. RIPS OVER BOTH KNEES -- I'm hot and go both ways.

4. RIPS OVER BOTH KNEES AND BUTT -- Do me baby!

5. RIPS PLUS SAGGING PANTS __ Go ahead!

SIGNS ON MEN'S BRIEFS AND LADIES PANTIES

1. HEARTS AND FLOWERS __ I'm hot!

2. NO PARKING -- I'm prim and proper

3. A BANANA AND FLOWERS-- I'm gay and willing.

4. Come On In -- I'm ready to go!

5. STOP -- Forget making any move on me.

How a naughty comic might look at the new high-tech devices:

ICONS ON THE COMPUTER SCREEN

File	storehouse of zany jokes, favorite DVD's by Lucas Entertainment/New Sensations
Calendar	where to note when you had an orgasm
Reminder	what to bring for your next hot session (rubbers, k-y, cock ring with vibrator etc.)
Notes	what you enjoyed most during your last hot love session
Maps	how to get to your lover's house or motel
Tunes	favorite love songs or music for love sessions
Books	romance novels, sex instruction books
numbers	times you got lucky and made love, e mail #s and cell phone #s of "hot" dates
Lunch pad	different positions and maneuvers to achieve orgasm
photos	photos of G spots, hot gals and guys

PIERCING

X

1. IN TONGUE

I can give you a blow job and riming that you will never forget.

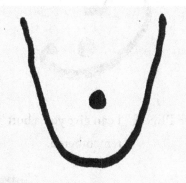

2. LEFT NIPPLE

I'm gay and ready for suck and butt jobs.

3.   LEFT EAR   I'm gay and with every action you may want.

4.   IN HEAD OF PENIS   I can give you a butt/vulva f-- that will be remembered.

TATTOOS

1. HEARTS AND FLOWERS ON LEFT SIDE — I'm gay and know how to please.
2. BUTTERFLY ON NECK OR LEG — I'm a tease and will consider an offer
3. BANANA OR SHARP INSTRUMENT ON LEFT SIDE OF BODY — I'm gay and into rough action

AN ODE TO ALL CLOWNS, IMPS AND ELVES

God bless all clowns, imps and elves
Who star in the world with laughter,
Who bring tears of joy to the audience
By their funny antics.

God bless all of them.
So poor the world would be,
Without their zany bits on stage which produce
Giggles, belly-laughs, and tears of joy.

God bless them all.
For their one-liners that make us laugh.
For all the slapstick that make us giggle.
For all the naughty things they do
On stage and in life to make us smile and chuckle.

God bless them all.
Give them a long, good life,
Make bright their way -- they're a race apart.
Magicians most, who turn their hearts' pain,
Into a dazzling jest to lift our hearts.
God bless all clowns, imps and elves

ABOUT THE AUTHOR

Buddy Alley, like his father Rodney, was a stand-up comic for over 35 years.

There for a while he was teamed with singer Nick Gorman. They enjoyed a lot of success with their comic, dancing and singing routines.

They appeared in night clubs throughout the U.S and in England and France. They were especially popular in New York, Chicago, St. Louis, New Orleans, L.A and San Francisco.

Buddy was also famous for his drag routines. He imitated Mae West, Marilyn Monroe, Marlene Dietricher and Liz Taylor. Naturally, he was warmly welcomed in gay bars and clubs.

Unlike his sister Shirley, Buddy never married. He was briefly involved with stripper Karen Moore (stage namer Pussie Galore) and had a son by her by the name of Sunny Alley. Sunny later went into show business as an exotic male dancer and stripper under the stage name of Peter Long.

Buddy is in retirement now,. He still lives with his life-long lover Raymond Montez who was and still is his valet. Once in a while he comes out of retirement to do one of his drag impressions for a charity.

Also, Buddy has made several risque CDs: "The Dating Game", "Burlesque", "This is Show Business", Gay-A-Go-Go" and his latest "Dicks and Pussies at 007."

This is me before my first gig with my parents.
Mom made my costume. I tap-danced to the
tune of "Yankee Doodle Dandy".

Goodbye From Buddy Alley

Well, here I am again with my little dog Taco. So long until next time when we can share some zany routines with you.

Until then, continue to smile, giggle and laugh at anything you find funny. Laughter lifts our spirits and keeps us healthy.

If there is nothing around you to make you laugh, get out a DVD of I Love Lucy, The Golden Girls, Are You Being Served, The Johnny Carson Show or any other great classic comedy show and enjoy a laugh.

All the folks on those shows were like us -- elves, imps and clowns.

Here I am as I am working on this book. Can you see my chihuahua Taco? I dressed him in a clowns' outfit.

Printed in the United States
By Bookmasters